To Jasmine and India

Inspired by my cheeky monkey nephew, Dexter

HODDER CHILDREN'S BOOKS
First published in Great Britain in 2021 by Hodder and Stoughton

Text and illustrations © Zehra Hicks 2021

The moral rights of the author-illustrator have been asserted.

HB ISBN: 978-1-444-95001-4   PB ISBN 978-1-444-95002-1

1 3 5 7 9 10 8 6 4 2

Printed and bound in China

Hodder Children's Books
An imprint of Hachette Children's Group
Part of Hodder and Stoughton
Carmelite House, 50 Victoria Embankment, London, EC4Y 0DZ

An Hachette UK Company
www.hachette.co.uk
www.hachettechildrens.co.uk

This book belongs to:

muceebeecighd

muceeiSdeenotcighd

CHEEKY
MONKEY

Zehra Hicks

Hodder
Children's
Books

Monkey play!

Do you want to play, Cheeky Monkey?

Your friends are here . . .

Zebra? Play?

That's my tail!

Play nicely, Cheeky Monkey . . .

Giraffe?
Play?

Meerkats?
Play?

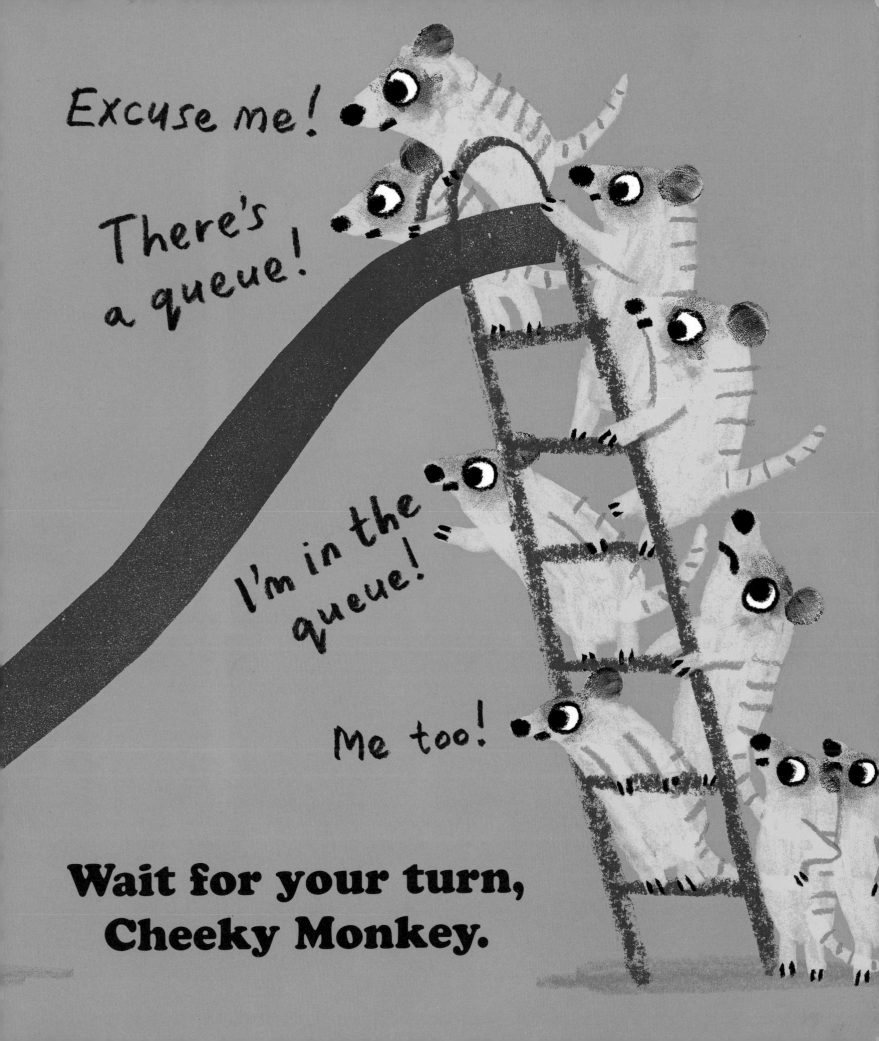

Ostrich?
play?

Elephant? "Play? ?

Lion?
Play?

Look out, Cheeky Monkey!
Lion is sleeping.

Oh dear, Cheeky Monkey.

What do you need to
say to your friends?

Sorry.

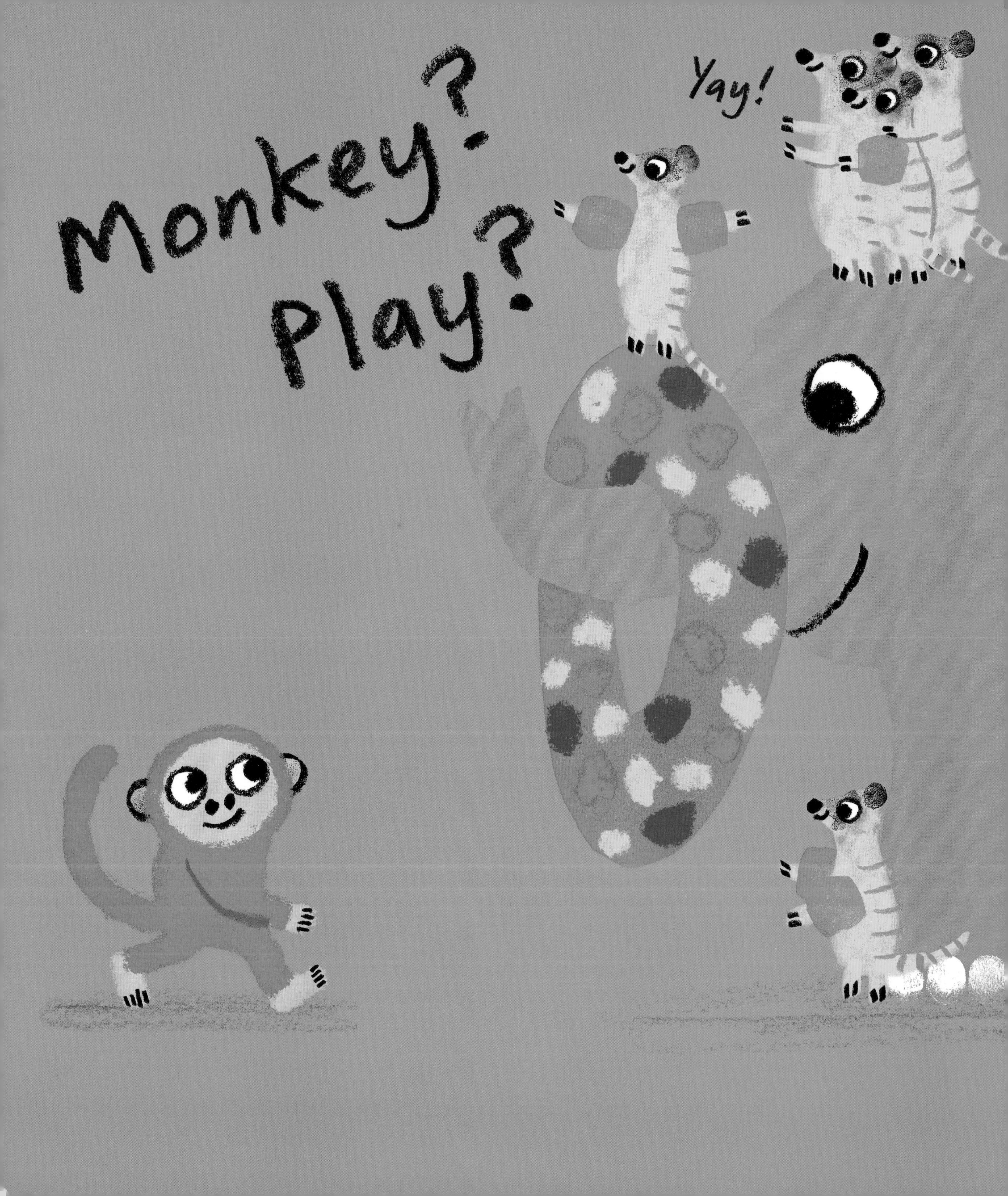

Monkey? Play?
Yay!

All friends together . . .

Everyone

PLAY!